W9-BRA-667

My Sister

Given to the Cairo Public
Library in memory of
Louise Hankins who loved
and cared for many children.
Nan Dougherty
Lucille W. Lutz

My Sister

by Karen Hirsch

illustrations by
Nancy Inderieden

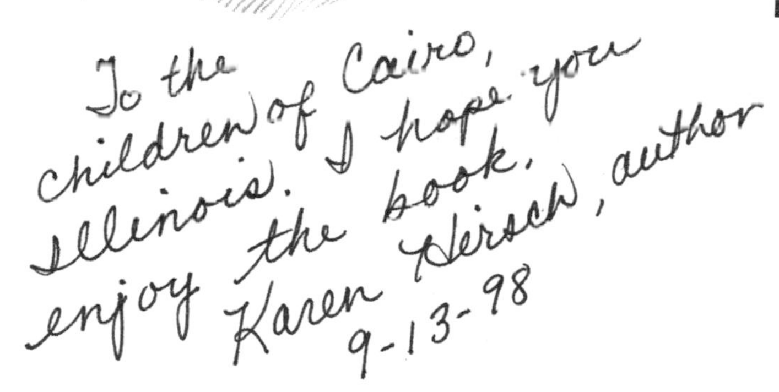

 Manufactured in the United States of America.

International Standard Book Number: 0-87614-091-6 Library of Congress Catalog Card Number: 77-74015

2 3 4 5 6 7 8 9 10 85 84 83 82 81 80 79

My sister isn't like other kids. She doesn't know many words, even though she is older than I am. And the words she does know sound scrambled when she says them. My sister can't stack blocks very high, and she gets food on her shirt when she eats.

My sister has an old teddy bear and an orange dump truck. She loves to play with them and hardly ever plays with any other toys. Sometimes I help her put her teddy bear into the orange truck and take him for a ride around the living room. My sister smiles then and laughs, and says, "Go ride. Teddy go ride!"

But only our family can understand the words.

My mother says that my sister's brain was hurt when she was born. She says that my sister will never be able to learn as well or as easily as I can. My mother says that my sister is retarded.

Every day I go outside to play. I ride my red two-wheeler and play kickball. I play with the girl who lives next door to me—she's my friend. We trace around each other on the sidewalk with chalk. We swing on the swings in the backyard and play in the sandbox.

My sister goes outside almost every day, too. She takes along her orange truck and her teddy bear, and she plays with them. Mostly I play with my friends, but sometimes I play with my sister.

Sometimes the other children in the neighborhood play with my sister, too. The very little children love her because she is gentle and kind. She pushes the babies in their strollers and shares her teddy bear with them. My sister smiles at the babies and pats their hair. My mother says that my sister is like a baby herself, even though she is a big girl.

Sometimes my sister makes me angry. I get angry because Mom and Dad are always helping her, always dressing her and playing with her.

Sometimes I think that my sister gets the best of everything. She has a big bedroom with three big windows. It is right next to the bathroom and to my parents' room. My room is small, with only one little window. And it's stuck at the end of the hall. One time, I complained to my parents that it wasn't fair.

"No, it isn't really fair," they said. "But your sister needs to be near us at night. And she needs to be near the bathroom, too. Besides, she enjoys looking out of her big windows so much."

So I didn't get a new room. But my dad and mom made me a bookcase out of orange cartons and painted my old room bright red and blue. That helped, and I didn't feel as lonely and angry as before.

Sometimes I get angry at my sister because she makes our family different. My friends' families have a good time together. They go camping and fishing and to museums. We go to museums and libraries, and we go fishing too. But it isn't as much fun when my sister comes along.

Once we went to the beach as a whole family. It was nice for a while. My sister pushed her orange truck in the sand and made truck noises. I helped her play, and we had fun.

But then my sister saw a baby on a blanket near us. She walked over to the baby, pointing and talking. "See baby, baby!" she said, but her words were jumbled. Just as she reached out to touch the baby, the baby's mother grabbed the child up in her arms.

"Go away," she said to my sister. "Don't touch my baby. You'll hurt her!"

The woman's face had an awful look on it. I ran to my sister when I saw what was happening. My mother came, too.

"My sister would never hurt a baby," I said. "She is kind and gentle!" I was very angry at that woman. My mother's face looked all tight and hurt. My dad said, "Never mind. They don't understand."

After that, the afternoon got worse. It was a terrible afternoon. Two little girls laughed at my sister and pointed at her. Lots of people just stared and stared. I was glad when we went home.

After that day at the beach, my dad and I had a talk.

"People don't understand that your sister is special and good," he said. "Most people aren't used to seeing a retarded child. They are a little afraid. But people who know your sister know that she is full of love and joy." My dad held me close then. I leaned against his chest and felt very sad.

I am growing older now, and I am learning new things every day. I am learning to swim, and I can kick a football. I can sing, and I am learning to play the piano. I know how to bake cookies and make hamburgers.

My sister is learning things, too. She is going to a special school now, with other kids like her. She is learning to dress herself and play games and say new words. My sister is learning to do things I learned to do when I was little. But she is learning.

I love my sister, and I'm sorry that she can't do things as well as other kids can. Sometimes I wish that my sister could be like other kids. When I blow out the candles on my birthday cake or when I see a falling star, I close my eyes and wish as hard as I can. But then I open my eyes and there she is, smiling and holding her old teddy bear. And then I know that she will always be special no matter how hard I wish. And I know that I love her the way she is.

Then I give my sister a candle from my cake and feel proud when she pretends to blow it out. Or I point to the stars in the black sky, and as she looks up, I see them shining in her dark eyes.

About the Author

Karen Hirsch is a writer and teacher who has a special interest in the education of exceptional children. In addition to her career as a nursery and elementary school teacher, she has taught classes for emotionally disturbed children and those with reading problems. Ms. Hirsch wrote *My Sister* in the hope that the story would help to dispel some of the fear and ignorance that surrounds the subject of mental retardation. The author received her master's degree in education at the University of Wisconsin in Eau Claire. She now lives in that city with her husband and two children.

About the Artist

Nancy Inderieden is an experienced artist whose illustrations have appeared in many children's books, including *The Dirty Boy, The Bridge to Blue Hill, All along the Way,* and *Being Poor.* Before doing the illustrations for *My Sister,* Ms. Inderieden visited schools for retarded children in an attempt to capture a realistic image of the story's main character. The artist received her training at the Minneapolis College of Art and Design and now combines a career of graphic design and illustration with photography and portrait work. She lives with her husband and four children in a rural community near Stillwater, Minnesota.

Published in memory of Carolrhoda Locketz Rozell,
Who loved to bring children and books together

Please write for a complete catalogue